NOTHING to do...

TRACY SABIN

Thar She Blows Books

Nothing to do...

Published by Thar She Blows Books
©2017 Tracy Sabin

Amazon print version
©2019 Tracy Sabin

ISBN 978-1-7938685-5-8

tharsheblowsbooks.com

Sarah and Kyle went to camp.

Danny, who is supposed to be in charge, is staring at his phone.

Charles is taking a nap.

There's nothing to do!

Who said that?

I can't play with the ball.
There's no one to catch it.

I can't play with the skateboard.
There's no skating in the house.

What did you say?

Hmmmm...

But... I don't have a canoe!

It's right there, silly!

That's my pillow...

Come on. Let's go.

Isn't this great?

Oh no! Whitewater!

We made it!

Up the hill!

Into the cave!

It's creepy in here...

There's a way out!

Wheeee...

Oh no! The cave of the googly-eyed monster!

There's TOO MUCH to do!

I'm going to sit and draw
quietly now...

Made in the USA
Las Vegas, NV
29 December 2023

83673943R00026